Erin,

Thank you for your interest in my short story. Take a good look at the cover, there's a lot of hints on it that will all make sense at the end of the book. Enjoy!

Melissa

MELISSA BLUE

Whitney and Wendell

The Revised and Expanded Version

authorHOUSE

AuthorHouse™
1663 Liberty Drive
Bloomington, IN 47403
www.authorhouse.com
Phone: 833-262-8899

Published by AuthorHouse 01/20/2021

ISBN: 978-1-6655-0021-0 (sc)
ISBN: 978-1-6655-0217-7 (e)

Library of Congress Control Number: 2020919066

Print information available on the last page.

Contents

Contents

Prologue

The sun shines bright and the weather is warm. A soft breeze is blowing in the air as the tree branches sway ever so gently. It's a beautiful summer day. Look at God's amazing creations! It's enough to put a smile on one's face. Exhale. Inhale. Take in the splendor. You're outside.

That's what the outdoors looks and feels like. But what's going on inside? What's happening inside the dwelling? What does home feel like? Is the atmosphere in there beautiful? Does the home feel peaceful? Is there joy and love in the home? Does it feel as if the Most

High's angels have been invited into the dwelling? Or is there only negative energy and darkness?

Come take a glimpse inside Roger and Missy White's home. Let's see what we discover inside their abode. Inhale and then release.

Whitney and Wendell

"Why have you come home smelling of alcohol and cigarettes?"

"I don't smell of cigarettes nor alcohol! You just need something to complain about, woman!"

"You do smell like alcohol, Roger; you smell as if you've had one drink too many. I can smell beer coming out of your pores."

"Missy, just go on about your business! You constantly nag, just let me be!"

"Roger, this is not what I signed up for! I didn't want to marry an alcoholic! You lied to me! You had told me that you only drink on special occasions and that you had hardly ever touched a cigarette.

Those things are not true, are they? You drink throughout the week, and you smoke a pack of cigarettes a day. You totally lied to me!"

"Fine! I'm a liar and you're fat! Missy, you don't even love yourself. Just look at yourself!" Roger began to walk as if he had a protruding stomach, mocking Missy's shape. He then started laughing at Missy while walking around as if he's pregnant.

Missy looked at Roger with disgust, and tears began to well up in her eyes as she tried her best to control her temper and actions. It became clear to her that he was not going to back down. It was clear that he had had too much to drink.

Missy turned to her daughter Elaine and told her, "My precious girl, I want you to go upstairs to your room. Go play with your toys. I'll be up there before bedtime to give you a bath."

Missy walked to her backdoor and stared out beyond her yard, far into the woods. She wiped away her tears as she opened the backdoor and stepped outside. Her backyard was very small, not even big enough to mow with a lawn mower, but she began walking around the perimeter of her brown, stained wooden fence. As Missy walked around, she took in deep breaths and then exhaled. It took everything in her to keep her head straight. Deep down, she wanted to strike like a rattlesnake, but she had her daughter, her sweet Elaine. Seeing her little girl's big brown beautiful eyes staring back at hers kept her sane. She had to be strong, not only for herself but also for her four-year-old child; so instead of striking, she walked and she prayed.

When Missy had calmed down, only seven minutes had passed. She walked back into her home only to find Roger looking inside the pots kept on the stove. Dinner had been prepared but his plate wasn't made. Roger stared at Missy as she made her way toward the kitchen.

"Ahem!", Roger huffed loudly in response to Missy not fixing his plate for supper. Although she heard him make that noise, ignoring him, she went on upstairs to check on Elaine.

"I don't know what he's humming for. The food is prepared. He's talking about my weight, yet he comes home smelling like a bar. There is no way I'm serving him. He must have lost his mind," Missy said under her breath.

After she had finished giving little Elaine her bath and getting her dressed in pajamas, Missy heard Roger walking up the stairs. He passed by Elaine's room on his way to the guest bedroom that doubles as his office. Even though Roger had a full stomach of supper, it didn't stop him from being a complete jerk to Missy. He walked down the hall, giggling and sticking out his stomach, still making fun of Missy's weight.

This time, Missy stormed out of Elaine's room and went straight into the guest bedroom. "If I am so fat and if I'm not what you wanted, Roger, why the hell did you marry me? You could have left me happy where I was. I would have never had to give up my life for you, for this hell that you have created!" Missy shouted.

Roger stood up from behind his computer desk and walked up to Missy and began yelling straight into her face. "You are the problem, Missy. Not me! You are less than the woman that I thought I had married. I should have left you right where you were!"

"I wish that you had!" shouted Missy. "I was happy there. I left a lot behind and lost a lot to be with you, but all you've done was lie and deceive me. How could you?"

"How could I? How could you? You're not perfect! You don't even love yourself! Lose weight! Get a real job! And then talk about me!" Roger yelled and walked away angrily.

Missy returned to Elaine's room. She grabbed Elaine and wrapped her arms tightly around her little body and started to weep.

"I'm so sorry, Lane, for all this fussing. I'm so sorry that you had to hear that. Mommy and Daddy should never fuss and yell in front of you. I'm so sorry, honey."

"That's okay, Mommy. It's okay. Don't cry, Mommy," Elaine said, trying to comfort her mother. She rubbed Missy's back and looked at her mother square in the eyes. When Missy saw the concern on her baby girl's face, she knew that she needed to call out for divine help.

Missy pulled back the covers on Elaine's bed and asked her to get in. She tightly tucked in Elaine. Grabbing Elaine's right hand, Missy knelt down on her knees to pray.

"Lord, I thank You for this day and I praise Your Holy name. Father God, I'm going through so much pain and disappointment right now, and a part of me is in fear. Lord, please watch over me and my daughter. Please protect us from any harm. Lord, I don't understand why these things are happening, but I do know that we need you. Keep us and love us, Lord Jesus. We love you and we thank you. In Jesus' name, I pray. Amen."

Missy stood up and called out to God once more. "Father, please send your angels to watch over Elaine." Missy then prayed to her deceased grandmother. "Grandma, I know you can see that I'm in a volatile relationship. Please watch over Elaine Grandma. Send some of our family and friends who are with you to protect my baby. Thank you, Grandma. We love you.

Missy kissed Elaine on the forehead and wished her goodnight before leaving. As she started to walk out of the room, she saw a bright blue light appear at the corner of the bedroom, near the doorway. Missy turned her head away and then quickly turned back toward the light's direction. The light was still shining brightly. It was so bright that Missy had to squint her eyes. And in a few seconds, it went away. She stood at the foot of Elaine's bed, astonished. She turned to Elaine and asked, "Did you see that? Did you see that burst of blue light?"

"Yes, Mommy. That was Grandma."

"What?"

"That was Grandma. Didn't you see her, Mommy? She was right up there," Elaine said, pointing in the direction where the light had shone.

"Oh my God!" Missy whispered as she held her chest.

"Good night, Mommy."

"Good night, Lane. I guess you're fine."

Missy was amazed at how calm Elaine was after claiming to have just seen her great grandmother. Not to mention the fact that her great grandmother was within or was a big blue light. Missy didn't see her grandmother at all and only saw the light shining at the corner of the room.

Missy walked out of Elaine's bedroom and slightly kept the door ajar. She looked down the hallway and saw Roger lying in bed all covered up. She was glad that he now seemed to be calm and relaxed. This gave her the opportunity to ponder over what she had just witnessed in Elaine's room. Missy sat on the stairs and leaned back against the wall, astounded.

Could her grandmother be giving her a sign that her request for protection has been granted? She couldn't be certain; however, she feels at ease with the occurrence. Although startled, she had no fear.

Two weeks had passed and life was still complicated for Roger and Missy. He continued to come home intoxicated, smelling of alcohol. Roger hardly came home straight from work, and most of his paycheck was spent at bars. Oftentimes, he hung out with his friends at the pub, running up a tab. Missy didn't understand why Roger needed to live like that, instead of being a devoted husband and a good father, but she figured it was best to say very little, just to keep the peace.

They're Here

ONE AFTERNOON, MISSY WAS SITTING in the living room, folding laundry while watching television, when she suddenly noticed that Elaine was having a full-blown conversation with herself. Elaine talking to her dolls wasn't out of the ordinary, but there weren't any dolls around, just crayons and coloring books. At first, Missy thought Elaine was talking to the TV, but a children's program was not on the set. Without putting too much thought into this, Missy continued to fold clothes.

All of a sudden Elaine screamed, "Stop it! That's mine. Don't do that!" Missy looked and saw absolutely nothing or no one Elaine could be talking to.

Elaine walked to her mother and found a seat on the couch in between the pile of clothes. "Mommy, please tell Whitney to stop messing with me. He's not playing nice."

"Who is Whitney?"

"He's my friend."

"Okay. Well, what is Whitney doing?"

"He's messing with my crayons; he keeps taking the blue one. I was coloring with the blue one. Not funny, Whitney."

Missy stared at Elaine with a puzzled look on her face. Missy had figured Elaine's imagination was just running wild until Elaine said, "Sit down, Whitney."

"Where is Whitney right now?"

"Sitting next to you," Elaine answered. A cool breeze brushed against Missy's left arm. Missy rubbed her arm as if she had caught a cold chill.

"Oh really!" Missy was astonished.

"Whitney and Wendell are my friends, Mommy."

"Whitney and Wendell? There are two of them?"

"Yes, they are brothers."

"Brothers? Where is Wendell?"

"Right there!" Elaine pointed toward an empty space. "He's standing in front of the TV, looking at us."

Missy's heart dropped a little to her stomach, but she managed to remain calm and not freak out.

"So I have two invisible boys in my house. This is interesting. I better ask more questions," Missy thought to herself.

"So, Elaine, you said that there are two boys in our home whom I cannot see and they are brothers. One is sitting on the sofa next to me and the other is standing in front of our television. Is that right?"

"Uh-huh," Elaine affirmed by nodding her head.

"Alright then. How old are these children?"

"Whitney is four and Wendell is almost six."

"What race are they? Are they white, black, or...?"

"They're white, Mommy. And you know what?"

"What?"

"Whitney has a red Spiderman shirt on and Wendell is wearing a green Incredible Hulk shirt."

"Really?" At this point, Missy was astounded. "What kind of bottoms are they wearing? I mean what kind of pants?"

"They are wearing shorts. Whitney has on blue shorts and Wendell has on green shorts. Stop Whitney!" Elaine yelled as she chuckled at her invisible friends.

"Do the boys have shoes on?"

"No. No shoes", Elaine replied.

"Humm, so what happened to them?"

"They died in a car crash on the highway with their Mommy and Daddy."

Missy's eyes grew big at hearing her four-year-old speak in such detail about these souls.

"So, they are like angels?"

"Yes, Mommy, they are angels and they are my new friends. They have been in my room."

Missy's mouth flew open as she recalled asking God and her grandmother to send angels to protect Elaine from the harsh conditions at home. Tears began to slightly well up in her eyes. She couldn't wait to tell someone about what she had just witnessed; so she called her friend Diane, who was a spiritual woman. Missy knew that Diane would understand. She had the amazing gift of being able to see angels and spirits. Her spiritual gifts were mind-blowing, kind of like a sixth sense.

"I want you to know that these two little boys were sent to you and the baby to protect both of you," said Diane.

"Wow," Missy replied with a smile.

"Yes. I can feel them and I can see a silhouette of their little bodies. My, what a bright gold light surrounds them! I can't see their entire face just yet, but I can see their form. They were sent from God and chosen with care. These two little spirits are very powerful, and they are not to be taken lightly."

"Oh my god!" shrieked Missy. "I prayed for them to come, Diane. I asked God and my grandmother to send help. Was I wrong to do that?"

"You did what you had to do, Missy, for your own peace of mind. I've told you on several occasions how powerful your words are, especially when you are emotional. You could call on an entire army of God's angels if you wanted to. He'll send them to you too." Diane began to laugh out loud. "Those angels will carry Roger's crazy butt right out of that house."

They shared a good laugh at the image of Roger being carried out of the house by an army of angelic beings.

"Your gift is amazing, Diane. We're in two different states and you can see what's going on in this house just as if you're right here. I'm blessed to have you to call upon."

"All will be well, my friend. Be strong and have no fear; your help has arrived so let them do their work. These spirits will keep Elaine's mind focused on being a child and not on you and Roger's marital problems," Diane reassured.

Thinking of the possibilities, Missy had goosebumps along her arms.

This was amazing, yet concerning, as she knew others wouldn't understand. It was challenging for Missy. But she knew that this was what she had prayed for; however, she wasn't permitted to see these spirits, only Elaine was.

Later that evening, Roger came home in a seemingly decent mood. Missy had prepared dinner and started to set plates on the table for dinner. Everyone sat down at the table to eat. But before they began to dine, Roger extended his hands toward Missy and Elaine for them to say grace together. Roger grabbed Missy's hand, Missy grabbed Elaine's hand, and Elaine extended her hand toward what appeared to be an empty chair. Roger stared at Elaine with an extremely puzzled look and then he shifted his eyes to look at Missy with a huge question mark on his face.

Roger asked Elaine, "Who's hand are you supposed to be holding?"

"Wendell. Will you please? Will you please hold Whitney's hand, Daddy?"

"Who is Whitney and Wendell?" Roger asked with the most peculiar look on his face.

"My friends. They are angels. They live here now with us, Daddy. Hold Whitney's hand so we can pray," Elaine said in the sincerest voice.

Roger extended his hand with hesitation; he did it for his little girl's sake. He held his hand with what to him was simply air.

"I'll say grace! I want to say grace!" Elaine said with excitement.

They always let Elaine participate in saying grace. Elaine was such a cute little girl and also quite lively. She was never afraid to speak unless she simply didn't want to speak.

"God, thank you for the food today. Thank you for Mommy's food, Daddy's food, my food, Whitney's food, and Wendell's food. In Jesus' name. Amen. Time to eat!"

Roger was a little taken aback and looked as if Elaine's imagination was in full blossom. Missy tried to hold back her laugh but she failed. She busted out in laughter, almost uncontrollably. Missy was more tickled at Roger's reaction than Elaine's new friends. Even Roger started to laugh.

"Y'all need to stop playing Missy. Y'all play too much!" Roger remarked.

"Roger, it's not me. I'm not doing anything. This might be a real thing."

Now that dinner was over, everyone would relax. Missy cleaned up the kitchen, while Roger went upstairs to freshen up and Elaine played with her toys.

Once Missy had finished cleaning up the kitchen, she and Elaine joined Roger upstairs to watch television in the master bedroom. Roger was laying on the left side of the bed, and Missy laid down close to Roger until little Elaine decided to get in between her parents. So, Missy scooted over and made room for her baby. Elaine hopped right in the middle of them. Next thing you know, Elaine told her father, "Daddy, move over a little."

"Why, Lane? You have enough room."

"Whitney needs more room, Daddy. Can you please move over a little bit?"

"I ain't moving over for no made-up children. That's too much!"

"Mommy?"

"Okay, Lane, I'll move an inch or two," Missy replied.

"Thank you, Mommy," said Elaine with much excitement and snuggled under the blanket next to Whitney and Wendell.

After Elaine fell asleep, Roger gently picked her up and tucked her into her own bed. Then, he walked back into his and Missy's room and closed the door behind. Missy looked at him like she knew he had something to say and she was correct.

"You shouldn't encourage Lane to pretend that her two little 'friends' are real Missy."

"I'm not trying to encourage her. For the moment, this is her reality. What's wrong? Are you scared, honey?"

"No, I'm not scared. But if someone else hears this, they are going to think that she's crazy. It's a little crazy though, you know?"

"Roger, look!" Missy pointed toward the closet. "It's the boys. Look they're right there!"

"I don't see anything!"

"You don't see them?"

"No, stop playing, girl! See what I'm saying? You play too much!"

Missy suddenly erupted with laughter. "I'm just joking. You should have seen your face!" She cracks up laughing. "That was so hilarious."

Roger found himself looking under the bedsheets, checking for a ghost. He really didn't believe that angels were in the house; however, he felt a little jittery.

The next day arrived. Missy was preparing to head out for a lunch date with one of her friends. Elaine was outside playing in the backyard all by herself. While waiting for Roger to come home, Missy decided to clean up the living room. Roger was kind enough to offer to babysit Elaine so that Missy could have some time away. As Missy was moving about the house tidying up, her telephone rang. She saw on the caller ID that it was her friend Tish.

"Hello, Tish," Missy said as she answered the phone.

"Hey, love, are you about ready to meet me for lunch at the Salad Bowl?" Tish asked. "I wanted to make sure that you didn't forget about me today."

"How could I forget about my bestie? Of course, I'm getting ready. I can't wait to see you! I miss you."

"Okay, just making sure. I miss you too! I miss you so much, sis!" Tish replied excitedly.

Missy and Tish have been best of friends ever since they were in middle school. They went to high school together and even the same university. The two were nearly inseparable growing up. In the 8th grade, Missy had come up with the idea of both she and Tish opening a bakery when they became adults. Tish had thought that was a great idea and so they had agreed upon a cupcake and cookie shop. The two of them had promised each other that before they grew old, they would own a quaint and cozy little bakery. Tish never gave up on the idea; she has just been waiting for the opportunity to seize the moment.

"I can't wait for you to catch me up on what's going on at your house. When you told me that Elaine was seeing ghosts and goblins, my mind was blown, girl!" Tish expressed.

"You are so wrong in that, Tish! I never said that she saw goblins! You really need to stop! Don't pick on my baby; that is so not cool!" Missy said as both of them giggled.

"You know I'm just joking; Lane is my little sweet pea! Seriously though, I'm looking forward to the chat. It's just an amazing story."

"Yes, it is," replied Missy.

"Well, is Roger being nice these days?"

"He's working on it. He's being nice enough to let me to hang out with you without having to pay for a babysitter today."

Missy then heard Roger walking into the house.

"Change of subject, Tish, he just walked into the house."

"Gotcha!" Tish replied promptly. "So, what is Elaine doing right now?"

"She's outside playing in the backyard with a whole bunch of toys thrown all over the place. She has like six dolls outside, a basketball, a hula hoop, and some more stuff. As a matter of fact, I should check on her right now."

With the phone still in her hand, Missy walked over to the back door and noticed Elaine playing with her hula hoop. But just a few feet away from Lane, she spotted the basketball rolling on the grass all by itself.

"What in the world?"

"What?" Tish questioned.

"Um, I think I'm seeing things because this isn't possible."

"Roger! Roger! Come here for a second!" Missy called.

"What's going on, Missy?" Tish asked anxiously.

Missy ignored Tish and continued to look out the door. The

ball rolled again, but, this time in the opposite direction. Elaine was twirling her hula hoop around her waist; she wasn't touching the ball at all. There were no apparent strong winds or any slope for the ball to roll down.

"Yeah, Missy, you called me?" Roger asked, popping his head out of the living room.

"Yes, come over here and look outside. Look very closely at the basketball over there on the grass."

"Alright, I'm looking. What am I supposed to be seeing?" Roger asked, approaching the back door and peering out.

"Just keep your eyes on the basketball. Focus."

"Missy, what in the world is going on over there?" Tish seemed more anxious now.

"Tish, give me a second and I'll tell you," Missy replied.

Roger focused on the ball and, sure enough, the basketball moved again. This time, it rolled about three feet.

"What in the hell am I seeing? Did that ball just move on its own?" Roger rubbed both his eyes as if clearing his eyesight.

"It sure did! I saw it happen three times now. This is really freaking me out," Missy replied.

"I can't believe my eyes. How is this possible? Let's see if it moves again," Roger said.

20

Roger and Missy both stood there staring at the basketball, waiting to see if it would move one more time. Meanwhile, Elaine did not seem to be fazed one bit by the unusual activity.

"Y'all are killing me over here! What is going on guys?" Tish shouted over the phone.

"Shush, just wait, Tish. A ball is rolling by itself outside."

"Are you kidding me right now! Y'all got some paranormal activity going on over there?"

Missy ignored Tish once again. She was intensely focusing on that basketball and so was Roger. Then, in a matter of seconds, the ball rolled again.

"Oh shoot! Aw, hell no! Missy, did you see that? The ball moved over to the left this time. I'm going out there to get Lane! The heck with this!" Roger shouted.

As Roger was about to take a step onto the back porch, the basketball moved abruptly. He and Missy then observed Elaine as she walked over to the ball and picked it up off the ground; however, they did not expect Elaine to say what she did: "Wendell, I want to play with the ball. You already had your turn, okay?"

"Oh my god. Unbelievable," Missy whispered.

"Lane! It's time to come into the house, baby girl! Come on now and get washed up," Roger called.

21

Missy opened the door wide so that Elaine could dart into the house with her dolls. Roger appeared a little shaken up, and rightly so, although he was not prepared for what was to come.

"Missy! What's happening now, sis? I'm kind of scared over here," Tish said with an unsteady voice.

"I'll tell you all about it at lunch, I promise. I'm waiting for Lane to come inside; here she comes now," Missy responded.

Elaine skipped past both Missy and Roger as they watched her enter the living room. She had so much life and was so full of sunshine. What a joyful child! Missy and Roger could clearly see that she was doing well as she pranced past them, but what they saw floating behind Elaine was unexpected.

"Roger, do you see what I see?" Missy asked slowly.

"Oh lord, Missy, what do you see now?"

"Look directly in front of you. Do you see them?"

With a quiver in his voice, Roger replied, "Them?"

"Look down, Roger," Missy whispered.

"What in the whole wide world is going on here?"

Missy then addressed Tish who was still on the phone waiting patiently for details about what was going on.

"Um, Tish, I'll see you at the Salad Bowl at 1 pm. I'm hanging up now."

"But! Wait, Missy! What's going on over there?"

Missy then spoke very slowly and calmly. "Tish, I have to go. Bye now."

She then hung up.

"There are two clouds of white mist directly in front of you, Roger. Can you see them now?"

"Yes, I see them. These must be dust particles from the sunlight. Yeah, that's all, just dust," Roger replied as if he was trying to reassure himself.

"I don't think so. I believe it's the children. The same children that had the ball moving outside. They are in front of you right now."

Elaine yelled from upstairs, "Whitney and Wendell, come here, I'm upstairs."

As Elaine called her invisible friends to follow her upstairs, Roger and Missy saw the clouds of mist transform into two orbs of white light. The orbs floated past the kitchen and toward the staircase. Missy decided to follow the lights and witnessed them disappear as they reached the top step.

"Do you still see the lights, Missy?" Roger asked in shock.

"No, they disappeared once they reached the top step. Roger, I'm convinced that we are seeing Whitney and Wendell. I'm pretty sure of it."

"I don't want to believe that we are seeing ghosts, spirits, angels, or whatever you want to call them. I just can't allow myself to accept it," Roger said.

"So, how do you explain the basketball moving on its own, huh? You can't explain that away. It is what it is, Roger, so just face it. We're not in this house alone. There are two male spirits here and they are young children."

"There has to be some scientific explanation, Missy. You know what I'm saying?"

"No, dear, I don't know what you are saying. I believe what I saw; I believe my eyes. I don't choose to be in denial. You can choose to act as if things are not as they seem, but I know this is real and it's definitely spiritual."

"Just explain this one thing to me then," Roger took a deep breath. "How is it that our child attracted these so-called angels? I mean, what is she? Some sort of spirit magnet or something?" Roger asked.

"Truthfully, Roger, it may be all my fault."

"How could it be your fault?"

"Perhaps, they are here because of me. I may have ushered them in."

"Missy, what are you talking about? Only Elaine can see them and describe them in their human form. You can't see any more than I can see. So, how could you have ushered them in?"

"Maybe there is more to me than you know. I can't put this all on Lane. I'll take responsibility for their arrival. Besides, it's good for Lane to have the company; she's an only child and needs playmates."

"You have got to be kidding me! Are you serious? Look at me in my eyes, Missy."

Missy turned to Roger and looked at him directly in his eyes. Roger could only look at Missy and shake his head.

"I'm going to check on Elaine, and then, I'll be heading out to meet Tish for lunch. I'm actually running late," Missy stated.

"So, are you going to leave me here by myself?" Roger asked.

"You'll be fine. You don't need to be worried about anything; besides, you don't believe they exist anyway."

She gave Roger a playful nudge and a smile.

A couple of weeks had passed and Roger and Missy were getting along just okay. They had some good days and some days were not so great. But there had not been any major blowouts and the house was peaceful and the atmosphere conflict-free, for the most part. That was until Roger went out with his boys on a Friday night after work. He came home drunk once again, smelling like everything that a bar had to offer.

Roger came home around 11 p.m. that night and entered the kitchen, where Missy was pouring herself a glass of water. He walked up to Missy with a grin on his face and commenced to hit Missy on her behind really hard.

"Hey, big bootie," Roger said as he grabbed her by the waist.

"Roger, you just made me spill water all over the counter. Oh my gosh, you're drunk."

"I'm not drunk." Roger laughed. He then went on to try to kiss Missy but he was being a little aggressive.

"Roger, stop it! You're making me uncomfortable."

"Uncomfortable? You're my wife. How can I ever make you feel uncomfortable?"

"You're intoxicated and you reek of alcohol. Please stop grabbing me. Please!"

Roger became angry and tightly grabbed Missy's waist and would not let go. Missy then mustered up the strength to push him back toward the hallway. Roger then stumbled against the wall.

"Oh, so you want to fight! You want to get ugly, huh? I'll show you ugly! With your fat…"

Roger attempted to move away from the wall, but he couldn't. He was stuck. It was like he was being held against his will.

"What? What!" Roger yelled as he slipped down to the stained concrete floor.

Roger looked like he was frozen in time.

"Rog, are you ok? What's going on?"

I'm…I'm hot," Roger gasped. "I feel really warm, I can hardly move. I…I don't know what's happening to me."

Missy suddenly hears a thump and notices Elaine sitting at the foot of the stairs watching the incident. Although she saw Elaine, there wasn't enough time to shoo her away. She had to make sure that her husband was fine.

Missy looked at Roger and saw him struggling to move off of the floor. She asked Roger once again if he was ok.

"I don't know what's happening. I feel so weird."

"Do you feel like you're having a stroke or a heart attack?" Missy asked.

"No. There is heat moving all through my body. Oh God, help me."

"Are you in pain, Rog?"

"No, I have no pain. I'm hot. I can feel it moving all over my body."

"Feel what moving, Roger?"

The hot light, it's flowing through me. Please help me, Missy, I can't move. Oh God!"

Roger could hardly catch his breath and talking was becoming more difficult. Roger stood five-feet-and-eleven-inches tall, weighing approximately one hundred and eighty-five pounds. Missy was much shorter than Roger, so picking him up off the floor was a challenge. It appeared that Roger was helpless. It was beyond belief that a man of his stature was being held down against his will by something that no one could visibly see.

"Let me help you up off the floor. Can you get up?"

"I'm trying."

When Missy helped Roger get up off of the cold concrete floor, he seemed to be able to move his limbs. He managed to get up with Missy's assistance and walked to the couch.

"Do I need to call 911 for you?"

"No, I think I'm fine. I'll be alright."

Roger's cheeks looked a little red, but the strangest thing was that suddenly he appeared to be sober. Missy noticed this odd change in his behavior. He was talking like a man who never had a single drink that night.

"Rog, perhaps you should go and take a shower, and get some rest," Missy suggested.

"Yeah, I think that'll be a good idea." Roger walked away with a straight gait.

Missy asked Elaine to come to her and have a seat on the tan-colored sofa.

"Elaine, did you see that?"

"Yes."

"Do you think that was Whitney and Wendell who stopped daddy from moving when he was pushed up against the wall?"

"Yes," Lane replied. "They made Daddy behave."

"Wow!" Missy grabbed her chest in wonder and simply took a deep breath. "Okay, baby. How are you feeling?"

"I'm good, Mommy." Elaine had a slight smile on her face.

Missy wrapped her arms around Elaine and hugged her tightly. "You're such an amazing little girl."

After he had showered, Missy went upstairs to check in on Roger. He was fast asleep, so Missy didn't want to wake him up. She just looked at him from afar, wondering with uncertainty about what had happened to him. Although Missy's concern for Roger was out of love, that didn't mean that she forgave him for his behavior. Missy was seriously on the fence about her marriage. She was tired of being on a constant rollercoaster ride and all the many disappointments.

On the next day, Roger woke up a little early for a Saturday morning. Missy heard him move around and the noise woke her up.

"Good morning, Roger. How are you feeling?"

"I slept well and saw a lot of dreams. It's not so much the dreams though, it's what I kept hearing in my sleep that's bothering me."

"What did you hear?"

"I kept hearing 'REPENT, REPENT' over and over again. It wasn't a loud voice at all. It was kind of quiet and calm at the same time. I woke up twice last night because of those words. Every time I drifted back to sleep I would hear it again after some time. It was like a dream, yet it wasn't a dream. Does that make sense?"

"I see. Yes, that makes sense, I suppose. What did you experience last night when we were fighting?"

"What do you mean?"

"You couldn't move when you were on the floor."

"It was like I could feel a strong force holding me against the wall. I tried to move, but I couldn't. The strangest part is that it felt like tiny little hands were on me."

"Children's hands?"

Roger looked into Missy's eyes and replied, "Yes."

"My God!"

"I remember feeling a kind of warmth going through my body. It felt like light traveling through my entire body. And you know what, Missy?"

"What?"

"I want to go to church tomorrow."

"Really? You haven't been to church in a year and a half."

"I know. I just feel it's time that I did. Yep, it's time. What happened last night scared me, Missy. It really did. Not only did it scare me but it woke me up."

"Okay."

"Will you come with me?"

"I wasn't planning on going to church tomorrow, but I guess I'll go since you want me to. I sort of had other plans, but I'll just cancel them."

In Missy's mind, she really wanted to stay mad at Roger—he had acted poorly with her so many times that she had nearly lost count—but in her heart, she knew God was at work. She could clearly see that it was only God's power that had allowed these things to happen. It wasn't easy by any means for Missy to humble herself, but for the sake of her family, she had to swallow her pride and be supportive of Roger's efforts.

On the Sunday morning, Roger was up with the sun—bright and early. He was already halfway dressed for church before Missy and Elaine could wake up.

"Missy! Missy! It's time to get up for service."

Missy awoke to Roger shaking her on the back.

"I'm awake." Missy was so exhausted that she could hardly see straight. "I'm so tired. Lord, please give me strength."

"He'll give you plenty of strength, baby. Come on and take a shower. I've already gotten Elaine up." Roger had a smile on his face. "It sure is a beautiful morning."

Missy was almost stunned at how her husband was prancing around the house and opening the curtains to stare out the windows. She went to get herself and Elaine dressed for church.

At church, Roger sat close to Elaine. He appeared to be a little nervous and Missy could see the anticipation on his face.

The choir sang beautifully, and the pastor preached a sermon that made the congregation dance with a Spirit-filled emotion.

"Trouble won't last," the pastor preached. "Weeping may endure for a night but joy comes in with the morning light. Church, do you hear me? It won't always last; don't you dare give up. Keep pushing and keep believing in God Almighty's power. He'll rescue you; He'll see you through."

The pastor preached the church happy and Roger sat there as if he had seen Jesus. He was truly moved; his eyes were full of water.

Missy felt better about going to church once she was there amid it all. She sang and praised the Lord along with the other congregants, including Roger.

Finally, it was time for the altar call. The pastor asked, "Is there anyone who wants to receive Jesus Christ as your Lord and Savior? Will you come to the front? Will you walk down the aisle and make your way to the altar?"

Roger sat there as stiff as he possibly could, almost like a board. His eyes were steadily watery, but he held his ground. He sat in his seat until the moment had passed. He didn't want to give in to the pull that was tugging at his heart nor to the pressure of the pastor's invitation. The pastor looked at his way at least three good times, but Roger didn't dare budge.

The next few weeks Roger continued to go to church, sometimes even without Missy. He even went to Bible study on Wednesday nights. For three consecutive weeks, Roger made his way to the church house. This was remarkable since Missy had the hardest time getting Roger to go to church for the longest time. He always had an excuse to stay home, mainly with him having a hangover from being out drinking with his buddies on Saturday nights.

On the home front, life was becoming more peaceful. Missy continued to have an open heart toward her husband since she could clearly see that he was trying to change for the better. Roger had been touched by two little angels; even though he wasn't ready to admit it, something inside him was changing. His mind was more on the Lord and that was a miracle.

"Roger, I have noticed that you haven't been drinking lately," Missy said with caution.

"I had a beer two weeks ago but only while shooting pool with the fellas. I don't know; my appetite for alcohol has changed. I was satisfied with having just one."

"Did Calvin and the gang seem a little surprised that you only had one beer?"

"Heck yeah! They were even offering to buy my drinks. I just didn't seem to have much of a taste for it like I used to. Man, I can't explain it."

"That's amazing, Roger. God is definitely doing something within you."

Missy walked up to Roger as he was washing his car. She put her arms around his waist and gave him a tight hug. He placed his left hand over her hands and gave them a squeeze. Roger turned around and took a quick moment to look Missy in her eyes while smiling at her. It had been a couple of years since Roger looked at Missy in that way.

Night began to fall as Missy stood at her bedroom window, looking out of it staring at the starry night sky. Roger was also in the bedroom, pulling an outfit out of the closet.

"Missy, I'm going to church tomorrow. Are you and Elaine going?"

"Sure, we'll be there. I might as well pull out my clothes tonight too. Oh, I've been meaning to ask you something. I felt you moving around in the bed quite a bit last night. Were you having a bad dream?"

"No, not a nightmare. But I did hear those words in my sleep again."

"Which words? The word 'repent' repeated over and over again?"

"Yes. This time I heard it seven times."

"So, you haven't asked God for forgiveness yet?"

"I've been praying. I'm not sure what else to do."

"Honey, God wants you to ask Him to forgive you for your sins. You know, for your wrongdoings or transgressions. He wants you to get saved."

Missy took a deep breath and exhaled. "Look, I've been tiptoeing around and trying my best to be mindful of what I say to you lately. The truth is, Roger, you have been an awful husband and not much better of a father when you're drunk. You've even treated your parents as if they were less than human at times. I'm so glad that you're drinking less alcohol these days, but when you were out at the bars, all that was important to you was drinking and hanging out with your drinking buddies; those are the only people that you showed respect to. So, yes, Roger, it is past time for you to get your life together. It's time, dear."

"I know. I'm going to sleep, okay? I need some rest."

"No problem, honey. Rest well." Missy kissed Roger on the cheek and turned off the lights to let him go to sleep.

Roger clearly had many thoughts running through his mind but didn't want to discuss them with Missy; however, Missy knew that he was being dealt with spiritually. The best thing for her to do was to not push any issue and allow the process to completely play out on its own.

The Day of Repentance

THERE WAS SOMETHING DIFFERENT IN the atmosphere—a feeling of hope. The house felt different on this Sunday morning; at least that was how Missy viewed things. She felt like something about this Sunday was unlike any previous Sundays.

"Good morning, Rog. I see that you are up and at 'em for church service."

"Good morning, my wife. Yes, I am. I'm happy about going to church today."

"It sure is a beautiful-looking day. The sun is shining bright, and the birds are singing right outside the window. What a lovely day. I'm going to go wake my Laney-poo up," Missy said joyfully.

Missy walks into Elaine's bedroom. "Good morning, Lane! I see that you're already awake."

"Good morning, Mommy. I'm talking to Whitney and Wendell."

"Oh, are you? What are you all talking about?"

"Well, Whitney told me that God wants me to be happy."

"Really?"

"Yes. And he told me that you and Daddy will be just fine. And you know, Wendell told me that a special star will shine bright tonight."

Missy was almost speechless at what she had just heard come out of Elaine's mouth. "Umm... Sure baby. We can look for it tonight in the sky."

The family made it to church and sat on the fourth row from the back pew, right in the middle; from there they could see the choir and all. The Spirit of the Lord was in the atmosphere and the praise and worship were amazing. People in the sanctuary raised their hands in sincere worship to the Lord. People sang and clapped; many had tears rolling down their cheeks.

What was it about this day? It was as if the Lord's Spirit made a special visit and poured His glory onto the people. It filled up the building with the glory of His angelic presence.

The pastor stood in front of the congregation and proclaimed, "The presence of God is here. Can't you feel His Spirit all over you?"

The congregants began to wail and worship the Lord even more. Some could hardly stand on their feet as the strong presence was too powerful for them to keep their balance.

"There is no need for me to give my sermon." Pastor Giles knows when to get out of God's way. "The Lord is doing all the work. The Holy Spirit is ministering all by Himself. There is no need to preach. Hallelujah!"

The congregation continued to pray and worship the Lord. Missy stood with her hands extended to the heavens as tears rolled down her face. Roger sat in his seat and cried. Something truly remarkable was taking place.

"If you want prayer for any reason, this is the time to come to the altar. This is the time people."

People flooded the altar following Pastor Giles' suggestion. The elders and ministers prayed for many people as they came to the altar.

Roger went up to the altar on his own with great speed, leaving Missy behind. It was like something pulled him up there. Missy saw her husband being prayed for, and he appeared to receive each spoken word. As the minister prayed for him, he nodded his head and wiped away his tears.

Once the prayer was over, the pastor directed those who had received prayer to go back to their seats. It became very quiet in the sanctuary, even the musicians stopped playing their instruments.

"If you would like to receive Jesus as your Lord and Savior, stand to your feet, my beloved," said Pastor Giles.

Roger, along with ten other people, stood up on his feet.

"Ask the Lord to forgive you for your sins. Repent children. Repent for your wrongdoings. We all fall short, children. None of us are perfect. We sometimes do things that are unlike God. We sometimes do things that hurt others. We occasionally do things to even hurt ourselves. Some of us break the laws of the land and some of us carry hate and unforgiveness in our hearts. We need to repent and ask God to make us over. We need to ask God to make us whole again. Ask the Father to remove all things in your life that are unlike Him. If you believe in your heart and speak with your mouth that Yahshua is Lord and that he died on the cross for your sins. Confess your sins. Tell God that you need Him and that you want to live for Him. Praise the Lord, Glory to His Holy name!"

Pastor Giles was old school and he went for a while preaching about the Lord. But he truly believed that from that moment onward, each of those individuals was now saved and sanctified: If people believed in the words that they confessed with their mouths, they would be saved.

The people in the church applauded loudly to celebrate each newly saved soul. All the new converts walked back to their seats and were being congratulated by their loved ones and/or pew neighbors.

Missy stood up next to Roger and greeted him by giving him a long tight hug. "I'm so proud of you Roger."

Roger embraced Missy and whispered in her ear, "I'm sorry, Missy, for everything. I've been a terrible husband. I'm so sorry, babe, for the pain that I've caused you."

"I'm sorry too, Roger. I forgive you, love." They kissed each other on the lips before taking their seats.

"Roger and Missy White!" Pastor Giles called out. "Stand up for me, children of God."

Roger and Missy stood up with a little hesitation and honored the pastor's request.

"I have been praying for the two of you daily for the last three weeks. The Lord has continually put you both in my spirit. God has much work for the two of you to do. He's healing all the areas of your marriage for a time like this. Whatever you do, be obedient to the Lord's voice and embrace your blessings. He's dealing with you." Roger and Missy received these words and nodded their heads in agreement.

The entire day was special just as Missy thought it would be. The family ate a delicious meal together and truly enjoyed each other's company. It was a feeling that Roger and Missy had not felt in a long time—such peace and calm. As night approached, Elaine went to her mother and whispered in her ear.

"Mommy, don't forget about the special star tonight."

Around 9 p.m., Missy, Roger, and Elaine sat outside on the trunk of Missy's silver Mazda 6 and looked at the sky. It was so beautiful and tranquil outside; the air was cool and the stars were plentiful and bright. At first, there was nothing out of the norm in the night sky, but around 9:17 p.m. an extremely bright flash of light appeared.

"Ooh! Look! Look! A big star! Look! It's sparkly!" Lane shouted.

"Oh wow. It is!" Roger remarked.

"It's beautiful," Missy commented. "Look at that one! It's flashing brighter than all the other stars."

"Whitney says God is happy."

"Yes, Elaine. I too believe that God is happy. I truly do," Missy responded.

Roger grabbed both Missy and Elaine and gave them a big loving hug. The star shined even brighter as the three of them embraced.

"I love you, Lane."

"I love you too, Daddy," Elaine said, as she smiled and looked into her father's eyes.

What a Sunday it was. One that would always be remembered.

The Time Has Come

A YEAR HAD PASSED SINCE THE glorious day that Roger made the decision to turn his life around and dedicate his life to Christ. The White's household was thriving and there was a lot of joy and love in their home. Roger and Missy's marriage improved substantially, especially since they decided to attend marriage counseling to keep their relationship on the right track. Missy was working on not allowing the memories of their dark days to spark anger and resentment in her heart, and Roger was putting so much effort into showing Missy love that she hadn't had the opportunity to relapse by being angry at him.

Roger vowed to stop smoking and drinking heavily. Every blue moon he would have a small glass of wine with dinner, but other than that, he no longer had the desire to have any beer or any other kind of liquor. Roger even got a new job and a pay raise working as a supervisor at a construction company.

Missy and her best friend Tish opened up a cupcake and cookie shop called *M&T's Sweet Treats,* just as they had promised each other years ago. Their business boomed, especially around the holidays. It was a lot of work, but they enjoyed every moment of it.

Little Elaine was now five years old and was excelling in kindergarten. Elaine hadn't seen or heard from Whitney and Wendell in three months; perhaps they had moved on to another child.

One sunny fall afternoon, Missy took Elaine to the neighborhood park to play before heading home for the day. As Missy and Elaine approached the swing sets, two little white boys were sitting on a bench directly across from the swings.

"Mommy! Look, its Whitney and Wendell!" Elaine shouted.

"What?" Missy asked.

"There! On the bench. Look! Can you see them?"

Missy could see two little boys sitting on the bench. She was so surprised to see two little white boys—one wearing a red Spiderman shirt with blue shorts and the other wearing a green Incredible Hulk shirt with green shorts. Neither of the boys was wearing shoes. Missy's mouth flew open when she realized that those were the same clothes Elaine had once told her Whitney and Wendell were wearing. And this time, Missy could actually see them for herself.

"Oh my God! It is them, isn't it, Elaine?"

"Yes, Mommy. They are here!"

The two little boys waved at Elaine and Missy, and they waved back at them. Missy couldn't believe what she was seeing. Once she and Elaine walked closer to the bench on which the boys were sitting, the two children all of a sudden disappeared; they vanished into the atmosphere.

Missy gasped, "Where did they go? They were just sitting there."

"Aww, they're gone now. It's time for them to go, Mommy," Elaine muttered in a sad voice.

Missy clutched her chest with her right hand over her heart. She was in utter disbelief. So it was all true; they were real and they were angels.

"They will always be with you, Lane; you'll always have them as friends, my sweet girl."

"I know, Mommy. God called them home." Elaine looked at her mother with a smile on her face and glossy teary eyes.

Missy held Elaine's hands tightly and said, "God, You are so amazing. You are so powerful, and there is nothing You cannot do. What a miraculous thing You have done. Thank you, Lord."

"Thank you God, thank you grandma and thank you Whitney and Wendell. Amen."

"Amen." Missy echoed as she smiled at little Elaine.

Both Missy and Elaine took a deep breath and exhaled.

A spiritual intervention took place in Roger and Missy's home, a home that was flawed and broken. Roger and Missy put on a spectacular front for society to see. When they stepped outside their home, they appeared as a well-rounded couple with everything flowing in the right direction. The family photos that Missy would post on social media were stunning. There, buried below all the likes and compliments, lay bitterness, pain, and addiction. Who would have known that Missy was a hurting woman and Roger was deeply flawed? As they say, you can't judge a book by its cover.

Their family was in trouble and in need of drastic help and, thank God, help had arrived just in the nick of time. There can be no darkness where light shines and Missy willingly, yet unknowingly, invited the light into her home. Angelic beings from the heavens above fulfilled their assignment and changed the dynamics of the entire family. Now, they could be at peace and experience the beauty of marriage and the joys of parenthood together under one roof.

Whitney and Wendell, well done.

The end.